The Polished Locket

The Polished Locket

Raven Lane

Print information available on the last page.

Rev. date: 08/24/2015

To order additional copies of this book, contact:
Xlibris
1-888-795-4274
www.Xlibris.com
Orders@Xlibris.com
707544

CONTENTS

Introduction ix

Chapter 1 1

Chapter 2 5

Chapter 3 10

Chapter 4 15

Chapter 5 18

Chapter 6 31

Chapter 7 41

Chapter 8 50

Chapter 9 59

Chapter 10 62

To my mother, although you're not physically here…I hope I make you proud by putting my best foot forward in all that I do.

INTRODUCTION

Thank you for reading my book. Regardless of our past and backgrounds, we're destined for greatness and can accomplish anything we put our minds to, with God first and hard work.

While writing, I kept asking myself, will I be a victim of life's circumstances? Or will I take positive control of my own destiny? This was the most difficult task I faced in my twenties-finding myself and the ability to gather all my trials and victories to author an adult fiction book that could inspire single mothers from different backgrounds. We each have a unique story that has placed us in the positions that we're in today.

Writing took time, tears, prayers, support, and most importantly boldness. Bold enough to share some of my story through the fiction character, Victoria. I knew I could encourage the next young woman that came from a similar background with no support, a single mother, struggled to support her and/or her children while trying to obtain a college degree, has had her heart broken from love, and traveled down some roadblocks while on her journey to success. This book takes you down the twisted paths in the life of a young ambitious girl that has fell for temptation and been misguided, yet she rediscovered her inner strength and determination to turn her life around.

My character Victoria grew up in Memphis, TN. As you turn the pages of this book, you'll discover some highs and lows of growing up in Memphis. Learning to adapt in certain environments in order to survive and most importantly, growing through it all to flourish into the woman you're meant to become. Of course, you'll never forget where you came from and you can't forget the hardships that made you stronger.

With growth, one must keep the love of God in their heart, and make the choice to live each day in the light of possibility. This takes strength and character and, most importantly, courage and determination to work to make a difference in you first. It's also difficult to be sunny and 70 (optimistic all the time) when things around you are a total mess. This story details how a young girl grew through so much in life, which helped launch her into the woman she became. Throughout the story, you should receive the encouragement necessary to release your strength, full of hope for progress. No one should have to bury it or fall into a platform of what others expect; instead, find yourself and began to embrace the individual you're becoming.

Writing has always been one of my many passions, and this was my year that I was determined to publish. With a humble heart, I have to show gratitude for your support on reading my book. While getting lost in a book, I also found myself in a book and most importantly I took from it an opportunity to encourage other authors that held on to their writing for years that if I can do it, so can you! Publish your work!

In order to be successful at any skill, your mindset has to be open for direction and think positive for change. Change is inevitable and can't be avoided no matter what, it helps us all grow. When the love of God lives within our hearts, we can all bounce back from any hardship. As you read the story about the polished locket, I hope that you receive inspirations to pass along to any young lady for words of encouragement that has faced similar issues like the fiction character Victoria and developed into a stronger woman.

CHAPTER 1

Saturday mornings were always busy in their household. Gloria got up early enough to cook breakfast and sit down to eat with her family before her long shift at the hospital. She was a workaholic that worked overtime any chance she could get. It had to be financially draining for her to support herself and five children…but somehow she managed. She would always remind her children that if it wasn't for the grace of God, she didn't know where they would be by now. Gloria was the glue that kept her family together and had to play the role of dad when necessary. She was only married for about five years to her high school sweetheart before calling it quits. He is the father of the two oldest siblings, while the other three never met or knew their dads. Victoria was the youngest of five, three sisters (Tia, Brittany, and Kel) and one brother (Ryan).

Phone rings:

"Vicki, are you riding with me to the mall?" asked Christy.

"Yes! I'm eating breakfast with my family now. I'll be ready in an hour. Ok, I have to go…bye." said Victoria as she hurried off the phone.

Christy and Victoria had been childhood friends since they were toddlers. Both of their families were close and always supported one another's gatherings. However, on Saturday mornings it was routine to sit and eat breakfast as a family. Victoria didn't want her mom to catch her on the phone during family time. During the week, they never had time to sit down as a family to eat together so Saturday mornings was their family time during breakfast.

This was the time Gloria made sure to know her children's plans for the upcoming week. Also this was the only time she had to catch up with everything going on in her children's lives since she worked so much. Victoria was the only child involved in extracurricular activities at school. She also was the scholar, and Gloria knew she would one day be the doctor in the family.

~

At school, Victoria received special privileges for her academic success. She was an all-around good student. This particular day Victoria was called to the main office to a teary eyed principal and other faculty with uneasy looks upon their faces. She knew something wasn't right; their looks alone had a distressed look on them. Dr. Johnson called Victoria into her office, Victoria slowly looked around and followed her into her office and took a seat.

Dr. Johnson asked Victoria, "When was the last time you spoke with your mother?"

"Early this morning, before I got up for school she stuck her head in my room as usual to tell me she loved me and was going in for overtime. What made you ask that question, Dr. Johnson?" Victoria explained.

"Victoria, do you have any other family on your maternal side?" asked Dr. Johnson.

"Yes, most of my mom's family lives up in Chicago and we have some relatives here in Memphis. Why?" Victoria asked as she sat up in her chair to view the television behind Dr. Johnson's desk.

"You're watching News Channel 7, we have more updates about the early morning car crash East Bound I-240 that left one dead at the scene and two others in critical condition. Stay tuned for more updates." the news anchor announced.

Dr. Johnson looked at Victoria, at that moment, her face alone held back tears of pain and sympathy for Victoria and her family.

"I'm sorry to have to tell you this, Victoria, but your mom was killed early this morning in a car crash." Explained Dr. Johnson while fighting back tears, she got up to put her arms around Victoria.

"No, Dr. Johnson....this can't be happening to me. Why would God take my mother?" cried Victoria.

The rest of the office staff came into Dr. Johnson's office to console Victoria. That day Dr. Johnson took Victoria home; her brother was there and had already received the bad news. He hugged Victoria and assured her that everything will be ok just like a big brother would console his baby sister. The other girls were on their way home; they got the call earlier that morning. Later that evening, everyone just sat around hugging each other and crying. They knew they needed to stick together in order to make it, because all they had was each other.

God will never put more on you than you can bear.

That night Victoria cried herself to sleep; thinking things would never be the same. She lost her number one cheerleader and only support system to keep her going when things seemed so rough. She was devastated along with the rest of the family, she couldn't be much help and the older siblings refused to let her get too involved with everything. They all wanted to keep her encouraged with academics just as their mom instilled in her. However, Victoria knew her older siblings couldn't handle everything they were facing with no guidance. They had to grow up and grow up fast.

Days later, the family gathered for the funeral followed by the repast. Gloria was 50 years old when she passed away and left a house and two cars to her children. From the outside looking in people thought this family was blessed with material things, but on the inside they were all broken and missing the glue that kept everything together. Victoria kept thinking how her mom spent so much of her time working to provide for them, their family time was limited because she was so busy making a living. Now that she was gone, how in the world is this family going to make it?

Always cherish time with your loved ones. They make remarkable memories and memories can never be taken away.

Victoria and the rest of her siblings were trying to keep things together. On the bright side, they received a lot of support from their mom's co-workers, family, and friends this helped take some of the stress off the oldest girls. Victoria took some additional time off from school, because she was coping with a loss. She didn't want to face anyone and answer any questions. She felt like the moment someone would bring up the kind words, "I'm sorry to hear about your loss." That she would break down. Her siblings thought it was best if she stayed home for a few weeks to relax mentally.

No matter what may be happening on the outside, you are in charge of the way you are on the inside.

Victoria pushed through her mourning and picked herself right back up for school. Reluctantly when she returned, to her surprise although her home was different, this didn't change how her childhood friends treated her. She valued these friendships with each one of them, because she knew she would keep herself out of trouble if she stayed close to young ladies that knew her best.

Easier said than done…

CHAPTER 2

Ryan had to sit down and have a talk with the family. He had got into a little trouble while gambling and playing basketball. He explained to his sisters for a little while he was going to move in with some of their cousins. The girls knew this wasn't like Ryan to hide from anyone; if he was gambling and lost, he would take his loss and pay up. Ryan was talented at playing basketball and street smart from experience. Their mom would always say if he would have had a male mentor or a coach in his life he could have went far with basketball.

Tia later found out that Ryan was getting around some of the cousins that always had a plan to make some fast money. Ryan was trying to take full responsibility of being the only man in the house; he didn't want to see his sisters' stress over bills so he stepped up. Victoria was worried for Ryan; they had just lost their mother and the last thing they wanted was for their brother to get into any trouble. Ryan moved out of the house and left his four sisters there alone. He always sent money to cover bills and a little extra to help out. The girls knew Ryan was coming up with a lot of money and fast money. It wasn't long before Kel got the call that they feared they would one day get. Ryan had been arrested in Houston, TX for drug trafficking and money laundering. This was his first charge; police also found a weapon in the car that he was driving which didn't belong to him. Their cousins tried to keep them updated with everything going on with his case. Kel had to break the news to the family, but she was also worried how they would be able to pay bills because none of the girls worked. Tia was a socialite in the Memphis night life, so working didn't go with her style on partying every weekend. Brittany was just trying to figure out which path she wanted to take after high school. She was always enrolling in school, then dropping out and never completing enough courses to graduate. While Kel was always in and out of town, she kept a boyfriend to help finance her. For the most part, she worked as a hairstylist at home on the days she was in town. With no financial support from Ryan, these sisters had to start paying bills to keep a roof over their heads.

A minor setback, but what happens if the comeback
takes longer than you anticipated?
Faith cushions your fall.

Victoria was trying her best to keep it together but she worried about her home and family. She was the minor, so if they didn't keep the house she didn't know where she would live and which older sister would take on the responsibility of caring for her. Although she still went to school every day, her face may have been in the books but her mind was on her family. Months after her mom's death and her big brother Ryan was arrested. She really couldn't talk to her friends about everything, because she didn't want their family business to get out in school.

A few weeks after getting the news Ryan was in jail, the girls were served a notice to appear in court for the ownership of the house.

Gloria was on her job for years before she had her 2nd child, their home was purchased during her first marriage with her high school sweetheart. While Gloria was young, in and out of love and mothering children she never changed the deeds on the house. Technically, the house the children inherited was left to the oldest sibling's dad. Since then he's re-married and moved to another state so he was fine with the children getting the house. He came to Memphis to visit them during the time of the Probate Court hearings. He embraced all of them with his love and support, even the children that weren't his. He told them not to stress about Ryan's situation, because they were already dealing with enough as is and needed to stay strong and stick together. He explained to the oldest girls, his biological children, Tia and Brittany.

"I never thought I'll finally see you young ladies all grown up and under these conditions. For years, I tried to get in contact with you all but your mother would never allow me to speak with neither one of you so I eventually stopped."

The girls believed him, because their mom held this bitterness towards him and for years she would say things like if he wanted to see his children he would come knock on that front door to see his girls. The oldest girl's dad was an old fashioned and hardworking black man. Except he was verbally controlling to his first love, Ms. Gloria, he didn't want to share her with anyone not even her family. He had a certain way he wanted her to dress since she was the mother of two girls and a certain way that she had to speak in public. That's why the marriage ended on a sour note which pushed her to purposely loose contact with him and sent him out of town to later re-marry.

The oldest girl's dad didn't dwell on that topic any longer, because he was more concerned with the children coping with their loss and receiving the support they needed to continue with life itself. He also tried to sit down and lecture them all, he explained they were going to have to get their heads out of the clouds and work to keep that house and stick together. He tried to help guide them in the right direction with going to school and getting a job, but the only two that listened was Victoria and Brittany.

When you grow up in a household with no male figure, it does affect the way a woman listens, respects, and loves a man.

By this time they all received a small inheritance package divided 4 ways, after a lot of their mom's debt was paid off it wasn't that much for the girls to enjoy but something was better than nothing. Somehow people talk and word travels when 4 young girls are living in a house alone with no mom and no big brother Ryan. People thought these girls had it made with a silver spoon in their mouth.

Victoria faced this at school, "new friends" suddenly wanted to hang out with her and asking a ton of questions and wanting to be in the know which at times caused her to stray away from her old friends. At times how old friends backed away, because she was dealing with things then that they just couldn't relate to and the friendship was probably too much to handle. To make matters worse, people talk and they began to hear negative conversations pertaining to their situation.

A little money doesn't change you; it changes the people around you.

Victoria started to miss a lot of cheerleading activities and hang out with the group of children from her neighborhood. She had so much on her mind; the last thing she was concerned with was dance. Although Dr. Johnson stayed on her about her academics, she still managed to produce passing grades.

One afternoon while walking home from school, Victoria caught the eye of a senior in high school named David. He drove a mustang and asked Victoria if she needed a ride home from school. Victoria didn't think much about it because she was tired of walking home every day from school, so she hoped in the car. On the ride home, David took the long route just to talk to Victoria. He mentioned that he was always into her, but didn't know how she felt about dating and knew her mom didn't really allow her daughters to date. He apologized about her loss and said he just wanted to be her friend. He also noticed that she stopped cheering at a lot of the games, and said because she was missing the team has been on a losing streak. Victoria knew David so well, and heard a lot about his scandalous ways and how he's instigated fights at school to have girls arguing over him. The question she kept asking herself, why did I get in the car with him? Finally, David got to her house and her sister Kel caught him in the driveway and told him to stay the hell away from her sister. He and Ryan knew each other from the neighborhood playing basketball together. Ryan knew what David was all about, and had previously warned all of his sisters to stay back from him because he's bad news; somehow Victoria missed the message.

Kel stopped Victoria in the driveway to explain to her how important it is that she keeps her head in the books to go away to college and stay away from the boys, especially boys like David. She also explained to Victoria that although she's always on the road, she does love and care for her sisters but she just has to travel right now while she's young. It seemed like everyone in the family was so busy with their personal lives they all forgot about the small family time that mattered the most. Victoria was very disappointed in her sisters, all of them…none of them were setting a strong example for her nor did she have one to turn to when times got rough. Although she was the baby, she wanted to pretend the oldest siblings could handle it all without her help but obviously they left her no choice but to grow up fast and learn to depend on herself. It was only a matter of time before this ambitious girl began to look for love and support in all the wrong places.

CHAPTER 3

From the car ride home and the lecture from her big sister Kel to stay away from David, Victoria did just the opposite. It had become a routine for David to wait on her after school so that he could give her a ride home. He was actually the one encouraging her to go back to cheerleading practice and stay focused on her academics. Although David had a bad reputation with women, he came from a good family. With so much time alone at the house, David and Victoria started to get really close, and fast. He introduced her to his family and they were officially a couple. Kel was away with her boyfriend most of the time and Tia partied so much she slept during the day like a vampire. Brittany enrolled in a community college and moved on campus. Out of all her sisters Victoria admired her and was very proud of Brittany.

One afternoon after school, David took Victoria to get a bite to eat then they got back to her house.

"Do you plan on going out of town for college?" Victoria asked.

"I don't know anymore, my mom has told me where I'm going, but I haven't decided." David replied.

"Well, what are you waiting on? You better make a decision, you're a senior." Victoria explained.

"Victoria...I don't want to talk about future plans with school right now. Why haven't I seen you dating any guys around school before me?" David asked.

Victoria replied, "I don't know, I guess because guys never approach me."

David replied with a smirk on his face, "Maybe it's you, Victoria."

David leaned over to Victoria and began kissing her. He kissed around her neck and began to unbutton her shirt. Although David was her first, Victoria wasn't shy with touching and kissing him back. He helped Victoria undress and admired her body from head to toe. He asked her to get up and walk around the room for him. Her caramel skin tone and tall frame definitely put ease to David's imagination of undressing her in his head.

Victoria was nervous, this was her first time with a boy and no one was home to interrupt. David pressed his muscular body against hers as he slowly began to kiss her. Without using any protection, Victoria could feel him inside of her. She was so caught up in the moment; she never bothered to tell him to wear a condom. Victoria thought, what in the world am I doing? If my mom was here she'd kill me! David knew Victoria was a virgin and no other guy at school has ever had her, he was determined to get her first. In the beginning, sex for him was like a game of chess; however, to her it was a moment of intimacy. After they finished, David stayed for the rest of the evening and the next day they both missed school.

Over the next couple of weeks, David and Victoria continued spending more time with one another at school and after school. Victoria thought everything her brother and sister tried to say bad about David was all wrong.

The easiest way for a man to get in a woman's head is in her bed.

She began to see him as this genuine and helpful gentleman. David started to buy her gifts and anything Victoria would ask for, he delivered it. He even began giving her extra money to pay bills around the house. He was the only person Victoria confided in when she faced family problems with her siblings. It was the same for David; he could talk to Victoria about anything. He always assured her that she was different from any other girl he's dated in the past. His mom would always joke and say things to her like her son must really like you because he's keeping you around for a while. Victoria really started to see the good in David.

David's senior year was coming to an end; he decided that he was going to go out of town for college after his mom gave him enough lectures to get his head in the right place. Apart of Victoria was proud of him for going away to college, but the other half of her was going to miss her boyfriend who's been there for her like a best friend.

~

A few weeks before David's graduation, and Victoria had gone to the doctor due to an irregular menstrual cycle to find out she was 6 weeks pregnant. The entire car ride home with Brittany was complete silence. She never told her the news; she figured she would get rid of it before anyone in her family would find out. Later that evening, David and her went out for dinner. He could tell something was wrong, she wasn't like herself.

"Is my baby already pouting, because I'm leaving for school in a few months?" David teased.

"Oh whatever, we have the entire summer together...besides I know you'll be home every other weekend." Victoria replied.

"True." David nodded.

That night he dropped Victoria off at home. She still didn't tell him, because she figured once he gave her some extra money she'll have the abortion and no one would have to know. Apart of her was so disappointed in herself? Here she was a scholar at school, mom just died and little support…how careless could she be getting pregnant at 14 years old? That night Victoria tried to pray and then cry herself to sleep. Brittany overheard her sobbing.

"What's wrong, sis? Talk to me." Brittany asked.

Victoria didn't say anything, she only cried on her sister's shoulder.

"You can cry on me, I'll hold you until you fall asleep…I know you miss momma." Brittany responded.

She couldn't tell Brittany the real reason she broke down; this was her role model and sister. Victoria knew Brittany would have been so disappointed in her. At that moment, she cried and knew she had to get rid of this unborn child.

That next day, David called to check on Victoria because he knew she wasn't like herself on the date. He came over and they decided to take a little walk through the neighborhood. This was so hard for Victoria to keep something so big from David. Finally, she mustered up enough courage to ask him.

"David, what would you do if you found out you were going to be a father?" Victoria asked.

David stopped walking and answered her question, with a question. "Are you pregnant?! Is that why you've been so quiet these past few days?"

Victoria replied, "Yes, 6 weeks. But David, I can't keep it. Look at my situation; I'll never graduate high school if I keep it."

David looked at Victoria with concern, "Yes you will…I'll make sure of that."

Victoria and David walked and had a long talk. He assured her that he would still go off to school and send money to take care of her and the baby. He also promised her that his parents would help as much as possible. Victoria's intuition told her this was the worst mistake she could have made over her life. David on the other hand was excited and making plans of how he can make this work for him and Victoria. Victoria knew his job at the mall wasn't going away to college with him. She also knew David's mom personally and she might not be that accepting to a grandchild. Her reality started to sit in that it might not be as good as David is making it sound.

Experience is the best teacher.

CHAPTER 4

That summer Victoria got a job at the mall and saved as much as she could. The summer break was over and Victoria was 5 months pregnant. Apart of Victoria felt alone, because most of her old friends on the dance team wanted to hang around her. She started to feel it was because she was pregnant, but the dance instructor would always assure her it was because she no longer danced with them. Assigned tables do exist in high school, so she no longer set at the table with the cheerleaders. Although she still had most of her old friends, she set around the other scholars. Victoria was still determined to stay focused on academics to ensure she graduated high school. She knew it's what her mom would have wanted and she also knows it's what's best for her future goals.

David's mom and her bickered, because his mom wanted her to move in the house with her. Victoria refused to leave her sisters and let the house go; she knew Kel and Tia weren't going to keep the house up as if their mom was still there. Finally, David's mom and dad had Victoria over for dinner. They made an offer for her that made it impossible for her to resist. Since it was David's freshman year on campus he didn't take his car, they offered to let her drive his car so she's not walking or catching a ride while pregnant. Then they explained to her if she moved into their house, the guest room was more than enough space for her and the baby. They wanted to make it as comfortable as possible for her and the new addition to their family. Although Victoria was hesitant at first, she talked it over with her sisters. Tia wasn't much support because she was all over the place with her life and men, rumors had it that she was messing with a drug dealer and supposedly his #1 customer. Victoria was in no position to get this girl in rehab and play the big little sister in her life. On the other hand, Kel stopped traveling so much in and out of town once she found out Victoria was pregnant. She was still doing hair at the house, but she wanted to keep the house to keep the sisters together. Brittany came home to visit any chance she could get, but she was so busy with school and advancing in the nursing program at a nearby community college. They were all very proud of Brittany, especially Victoria. Brittany told Victoria that she wanted her to move in with the Tucker's (David's mom and dad); because none of the girls knew anything about raising a baby and it would be best for her. She gave her the assurance that she shouldn't stress over the household responsibilities, because her big sisters got it.

Victoria decided to take the offer and move in with the Tucker's. She realized how much easier they made it work for her academically; however, she missed her sisters and her house. It didn't quite feel like home, she couldn't really get comfortable because it wasn't home for her. Although in the beginning, David enjoyed it because when he returned home he was able to see her. David would always assure her that everything will be okay and once she has the baby, she would see how supportive his family will be.

"Stepping onto a brand new path is difficult, but not more difficult than remaining in a situation, which is not nurturing to the whole woman" –Maya Angelou

The guidance counselors and Dr. Johnson were very resourceful for Victoria's circumstances. They were always trying to tell her different resources available to her and making sure her grades were kept up. The time had finally come for Victoria to have her baby. It was also the end of the first semester for David, so he was home but wasn't the same. Victoria started to notice the change in David's behavior after the first days being home. It was as if she annoyed him by being in his space and when he would get on the phone he would leave the room. For the most part, David was still very reliable when it came to taking care of his responsibilities she tried not to sweat the small stuff.

During the last few weeks of her pregnancy, Victoria was very tired and used that time to catch up on as much rest as possible. Mrs. Tucker was preparing the house for the baby. While Mr. Tucker worked overtime to ensure they were financially prepared for the new addition. This was different from growing up in a single parent household where most of the work is on one parent. Victoria was also beginning to look on the bright side of things and not worry so much about her situation because she had support. Victoria was optimistic about David and her relationship after the baby, because she saw the example his parents set for him.

It was December 11, 2003; Victoria and David were officially parents to a healthy baby boy weighing 7 lbs. and 11 ounces. They named him Parker. After giving birth to Parker, Victoria felt some stress lift off her shoulders and every small worry no longer troubled her. She pushed out some motivation to give her the encouragement to continue to grow and go back to school to make the best out of being a teen mom.

In the delivery room, David asked, "What's wrong?"

Victoria cried tears of joy, "I remember I wanted to abort this unborn child. Just looking at his innocent face, I'm so grateful to have him. He came out of me and God trusted me enough to raise him. I'm just so thankful right now."

David hugged her and said, "I told you that it'll work out."

Nobody can make it in this world alone.

CHAPTER 5

It was the end of Victoria's sophomore year in school, after having the baby she went back to school but missed a lot of days due to abdomen complications. If it wasn't for the grace of God, she would have never made it with a new baby and school work.

Things at the Tucker's house weren't as smooth as they were before. Mr. & Mrs. Tucker were having marital problems and at times, this affected how impatient Mrs. Tucker was becoming with Victoria and the new baby. Mrs. Tucker would have girl talks with Victoria just as if she were her daughter. David had an older brother away in the army, but no sisters. She was very meticulous about things Victoria did in the house or for the baby. Victoria enjoyed the bond Mrs. Tucker and she shared; however, she had to be limited on what she shared with Mrs. Tucker because this was David's mom. She also found her hovering mother traits slightly annoying at times. Funds were also getting tight in the household and a few times it was mentioned to Victoria to get a job. Although the babysitting was convenient and financial support helped her, but reality started to sit in with Victoria that this wasn't as easy as David made it sound.

She tried to reach out to him and talk just to keep their relationship like it used to be, but it would never be the same because David wasn't the same. It was rumored around school that David was playing basketball on campus and was now getting looked at by coaches and recruiters. He was starting to grow on the college campus, and forgot about his responsibilities at home.

One weekend, Mrs. Tucker and Victoria went to visit him. Victoria saw something she was not expecting, a crowd of girls around him and he didn't move once he saw Victoria with the baby.

Mrs. Tucker whispered to Victoria, "Don't be insecure sweetheart; he's just being a man. David loves you and his son; he wouldn't do anything foolish to jeopardize what he has at home."

Victoria nodded her head in agreement. However, on the inside she was furious that she was even expected to play the silent mother while he "grew as a man". She wanted to kick David's ass in front of his mom, the groupies, their son, and whoever else saw and could hear her rage. She was boiling on the inside, but Mrs. Tucker was a great mentor/mother with grooming Victoria. She knew if she would have acted out of rage how unladylike she would have looked and how disappointed she would have been in herself. For a 16 year old teen mother, she kept it together!

Mrs. Tucker politely said to him while Victoria walked away to sit down, "Son, get over here to see your woman and son! I didn't spend all that time on the highway to get up here and fuss at you."

David escorted Victoria and his mom to his dorm room. Once they were in the room, he hugged the both of them and kissed Victoria assuring her that was nothing you saw and please don't overthink it. David always had a way with words and a great sense of humor. He was indeed a charmer; he eventually cracked a few jokes to have his two favorite girls laughing at everything he said. Later that evening, they all went to lunch and Mrs. Tucker took her grandson to give Victoria and him some time alone.

"I've missed you like you crazy." David said.

"Really. Yeah, I've missed you too. I've been so busy with school, raising the baby, and now I have to find a job. David, it's a full load on a 16 year old. I'm trying to hang in there, but I can feel your parent's frustration with me living there." Victoria explained.

"No, it's not you. It's a lot going on in my family that they're not going to share with you. My parents are having marital problems and my scholarships didn't cover all of my tuition as expected. They're happy to help with their grandson; it's just a lot on them. Where have you applied for work?" David asked.

"Well, I haven't I figured I'll go back to the mall to work after school." Victoria answered.

"That'll be good. Hopefully, I can make the basketball team up here and the coach mentioned that he'll work on trying to get me a partial scholarship. I'll take it, something is better than nothing." David laughed.

"True, you better take it and you try to go as far as possible with basketball. Don't leave me and the baby!" Victoria joked with him.

David laughed at her, "Yeah, you're crazy if you think a man would leave his best friend, mother of his son, and woman for groupies."

Although David and Victoria were in a long distant relationship, this didn't change their bond. When they got together, it was like they picked up as if the friendship never ended. Whenever David had Parker in his arms, he would lay him on his chest and keep his little man close to his side. Victoria admired so many of the good qualities David always showed her that he had in him.

Victoria had a full schedule: school during the day, worked part-time hours 6 days a week was a single mother by night and on her off days, and the guidance counselors kept her involved in some scholastic activities at school. They assured her this will help her academically in the future and the involvement looks great on college applications and just for your own personal growth. Everyone saw how hard of a worker Victoria was, and they recognized her potential. They knew she was smart and strong enough to finish high school and advance to any college of her choice, if she kept her grades up.

Time passed and the baby grew fast. She rarely had time for her sisters, friends, and not even enough time to check on David. She had become a walking zombie. Every now and then Christy would check on her and the baby. Although their friendship wasn't like it used to be, because time changed it. Christy still valued their years of friendship and bonds previously set by their families.

It was time for Parker's 1st Birthday. Mrs. Tucker teased Victoria, because she couldn't tell who was more excited Victoria or David. Once David got home, he had brought bags of clothes for Parker and gave money to his parents and Victoria. Although David wasn't working, he never mentioned to them if he had made the team. Apart of her wondered where he had gotten the money from for all of this stuff, but there were too many activities going on in the house for Parker's 1st Birthday to even ask.

After the birthday party, David and Victoria wanted to spend some time together. His mom watched Parker while they went out. It had been so long since the two of them had a date being they were in a long distance relationship. Some of David's friends from college were in town and spotted the two of them out. David introduced Victoria to his friends as his fiancé.

By the end of the night, David got back to his parent's house and told her to go in the house because he had some errands to run.

"David, what are you up to?" Victoria asked.

David answered, "Nothing, just go in the house."

He leaned over to kiss her, got out of the car to open her door, and walked her to the front door.

He jokingly said, "I'll bring you back some snacks...you want ice cream or cookies?"

Victoria didn't laugh, this time she didn't find his humor so charming because David was keeping something from her.

Before closing the door, Victoria said "No thank you, David, I don't want any snacks. Be careful."

~

David met up with his friends that were home from school. He parked his car in a vacant parking lot and got in the car with his homeboy Q. They had known of one another in the neighborhood, but recently got back connected with each other from being away at college.

"Man, I didn't know you were that serious with your baby momma. You introduced her as your fiancé. Are you getting married, bro?" Q asked.

David replied, "Hell no, I just say that in front of her. She's really sweet and I was her first, when I got her pregnant moving her in with my family really helped her situation out a lot. She isn't going anywhere."

Q laughed and shook his head, "David, the beast...my man!"

David and Q went out to the grand opening of a night club in Memphis. Since David had started playing basketball at college, he had met a lot of people from the courts and in different cities. When he got back to Memphis, every girl either knew of David or wanted to get to know David. That night he never came back home.

The next morning, Victoria got up and got ready for work. They were out of school for Christmas/New Year's break. She thought David would be home in time to watch his son while she went to work, but he wasn't. Mrs. Tucker always covered for him, she told her not to worry about anything because she'll keep her grandson. She would always try to find positive encouraging words to soothe Victoria's frustrations. Since Mrs. Tucker had technically taken

Victoria under her wings like her daughter and raised her like the daughter she never had, she always tried to keep the peace between David and Victoria. Victoria started to observe how Mrs. Tucker was in her own marriage, a part of her hated that this woman never spoke up for herself. She was starting to become a mini Mrs. Tucker, except she was only 16 years old and David was the only guy she had been with.

~

Victoria and Brittany made time to go to lunch during both of their busy schedules. Brittany would tell her how hard nursing school is, but how much she loves the challenge and is eager to one day work in that field. Victoria would listen in amazement, because she knew she was going to follow Brittany's footsteps.

Brittany would tease her about being their mom's baby and favorite, "Mom, thought you would be the only one to go to school. I guess because you were the only one whose dad had a head on his shoulders and was a well-known doctor and polygamist." Brittany grabbed her own mouth.

"What, did you just say?" Victoria asked.

"Nothing, finish eating. You have to get back to work." Brittany said in a hurry, "Waiter, check please."

"No, what did you just say about my dad? My daddy was a doctor? My mom was the mistress? HELLO, Brittany!" Victoria said without shouting too loud.

"Look at you, Mrs. Tucker has refined you into the perfect future wife for her son. Silent, beautiful, smart, hard-working, ambitious, goal-oriented, driven, and can multi-task with baby Parker on your hip." Brittany said.

"Where is all of this coming from, Brittany?" Victoria asked.

"Sister, once I finish nursing school and my finances are straight you're coming to live with me. It'll be so much better for you. I know I told you to live with the Tucker's because for right now it's what's best for you…but look at how she's pruning you. You're only 16 years old…you can't even hang out with any of your friends." Brittany said with an attitude.

"Well, Brittany, my life has changed and isn't the same as my former friends. Never mind, you wouldn't understand…I guess maturity doesn't come with age." Victoria said.

"No, children mature you but it is best if you get with your family like your sisters when the time is right. I'm not able to take you in now, and I have enough sense to not send you to Tia and Kel. Trust me, maturity does come with age and I'm only trying to do what's best for you and my nephew, Parker. That's why I work so hard in nursing school, because I have you two to look after and you're going to college like momma would have wanted." Brittany said with a stern voice.

After Victoria's lunch date with Brittany, it put something else on her mind. She was becoming so passive to everything, because of Mrs. Tucker but also because she was still a girl. She couldn't use her voice now; she felt like she needed them until she finished school. Then she felt like once she graduates high school, she'll need Brittany's support to get her through college until she's in her profession. Victoria did something she hadn't done in a while and that was talk to God, she began to pray more and just ask him to give her strength and guidance where she learns to trust and depend on him. She knew if she was going to pray, she had to believe and have faith that God knows what's best for her.

"So those who have faith are blessed along with
Abraham, the man of faith." Galatians 3:9

David finally returned home from the previous nights, he brought Victoria a nice designer bag and some shoes. She accepted it, but knew it came with a price tag to cover her voice and emotions to avoid arguing with him. Victoria just wanted to love and hold on to her baby boy Parker. Aside of her wanted to break down and cry, just for the overload of life itself yet she had no shoulder to cry on so she sucked it up.

Victoria started to pick up more hours at work, just to stay out of the Tucker's house as much as possible. She was also saving, she knew once she finished high school that she was going to have to move again so she better save while she can. Any money David would send her and give to her, instead of her shopping, she began putting it away for a rainy day. Finally, it was the end of Victoria's junior year in high school. She had been accepted into the National Honor's Society with the support of the guidance counselors staying on top of her. That summer she started taking practice exams for the ACT, she was behind because most of her classmates had taken it during the school year. She started to put less effort into going to work so much, because she was preparing herself for her senior year in high school and knew she wanted to go off to college.

~

One particular afternoon at work, Victoria bumped into a young man from school. He was in the Engineer's club, Victoria didn't know him but he knew her. He told her that he admired some of her work that one of her previous teachers shared with the class. She thanked him and started to walk towards the mall's exit. He continued following her in the mall and talking. She wasn't rude; she didn't mind the small conversation with him.

Victoria stated, "I'm sorry…your name…."

"Anthony!" the young man answered.

"Yes, Anthony, that's right…I remember you." Victoria replied.

"I just wanted to tell you that I think you're really smart and pretty. Dr. Johnson always brags on you in the office. I'm one of the office assistants." Anthony added.

"Thank you, Anthony. I've seen some of your work in the library near the Young Engineer's section. That sounds like a complicated field, but you make it look easy. I'm sure your family is very proud of you." Victoria said.

Anthony blushed and nodded his head before walking off extremely fast. Victoria thought that was pretty weird how he abruptly ended their conversation. By the time Victoria reached the mall's exit door, she saw Mrs. Tucker through the glass window shaking her head in disappointment.

"Now Victoria, you're a mother now and my son's woman. How do you think that would make my son feel if he had seen you flirting in the mall with all those men around you?" Mrs. Tucker stated.

Victoria laughed to keep from yelling and politely told her, "Mrs. Tucker, I wasn't flirting…I don't have to. That was a classmate from school."

Mrs. Tucker looked at Victoria and asked, "Are you smelling yourself young lady? You don't have to flirt." Mrs. Tucker laughs and said, "Don't bite the hand that feeds you."

At that moment, Victoria knew her living situation was going to have to change. She and David were not on the best terms, and his mother is taking her mentor job too serious to Victoria's liking. All Victoria wanted was the love and support from her sisters, who weren't able to give it to her at that time. At home, she began to get rebellious towards Mrs. Tucker and the only time her and David saw each other was when he came home bearing gifts like Santa. Here Victoria was, a 17 year old and experiencing so much in this short time period of her life. She had to learn early how to pray and stay consistent in prayer.

~

The summer had passed and Victoria had taken a short getaway to a waterpark with Parker and Christy. For the most part, Christy was still her friend trying to be there for her except Victoria kept so much from her and thought she would find it hard to relate to anything she had going on in her life. However, they always made the best out of the time they could spend together as friends.

Christy was the type of friend that was good to the surface of being good, but great at being bad. She was so much fun to be around, and Victoria missed the good times they shared together as friends. Christy made sure not to leave out any details of what was going on in her life. Christy had lost her virginity way before Victoria. Victoria was kind of shocked that she never got pregnant. It was a blessing in disguise for Victoria to have a friend like this, because she was the one that taught Victoria about taking birth control and keeping condoms just in case the guys tell you that he doesn't have any. She stayed on Victoria about practicing safe sex, because she didn't want to see Victoria end up with more children by David at this time in her life.

Christy said, "So I'm dating a football player at Worchester Jr. College. He has a friend…that I think would be a great match for you."

Victoria replied, "What about David and me living at the Tucker's house?"

Christy added, "What about it? You're trying to move right? If you got your own apartment during our senior year in high school, we would have so much fun over there and can have parties too!"

Victoria looked at Christy, "Really?! You get an apartment. Or move in with my sisters? Tia would love to take you under her wings."

Christy laughed at the thought, "Oh no, let me shut my mouth. My mistake, you stay at the Tucker's until you finish high school."

Victoria added, "Right!"

"But you can still have a little something on the side. My mom always taught me not to put all your eggs in one basket. Plus David is away at college, you know he's…never mind" Christy jokingly stated.

Victoria replied, "Please don't say that! Even though I know it's true...how tall is that friend again? Does he play football too?"

Christy laughed, "Yep, let's have some fun! Just tell Mrs. Tucker that you're studying with some group members in the National Honor's Society after school and skip work. I'm sure he's willing to pay to have a fox like you on his arm a few days out of the week. And you can still save to move out when you get to college."

"Sounds easy let me think about it. Did I tell you the guy over the Engineer's club at school, Anthony, stopped me in the mall and we started small conversation. As we were walking out, Mrs. Tucker saw me once I got to the exit and told me that I was a little flirt and ran the boy off." Victoria shared and began laughing, "I wasn't even flirting."

Christy added with laughter, "Yes, she should worry more about Mr. Tucker...never mind I won't be messy, but don't let that get next to you. She's just trying to keep you around for David's sake, because she knows her son takes after his dad and needs a young lady like you."

Victoria was slightly torn and a sucker for love and charm, "But that's a good thing, right?!"

Christy replied, "WRONG! When you're 30, maybe? Maybe, even if you both were on the same page in the relationship that would be a great thing. Since you're not, it's not a good idea for a 17 year old to lose her voice....that is a ridiculous plan for self-destruction."

Christy and Victoria both ended the conversation in agreement.

~

David and Victoria rarely spoke to each other on a regular basis, except when it was time to drive up and visit him their relationship was still there. He was still this charming gentleman that loved his mom, "fiancé", and son. He finally announced that he made the basketball team and that helped his parent's out a lot with covering his tuition. Everyone was so proud of him. By now Parker was 2 years old and starting to resemble David. This particular visit was nothing like all the other visits. Victoria remembers how a young lady approached her asking if she was David's sister? Of course, she told her no and Mrs. Tucker gave her a speech about how technically we are all brothers and sisters in the eyes of God. Victoria started to become annoyed by Mrs. Tucker and her entire situation ship. She was ready to call it quits, and remembered what Christy told her.

"David, can I speak with you in private?" Victoria politely asked.

David answered as he took Victoria's hand and walked with her, "What's going on baby?"

"David, I've been really patient with this entire set up. Living with your parents, coming up here to visit you with your mom, being a sweet great girlfriend, but David I am a little tired with the long distant relationship." Victoria explained.

David replied, "So you breaking up with me?"

"I just think I want to move back in the house with my sisters until I graduate and go off to college." Victoria added.

David nodded his head and said, "Victoria, don't be stupid baby. Living with my parents is helping you out. If you move back in with your sisters they are going to stress and work the hell out of you with paying bills. Listen to me, stay with my parents at least until you finish high school. My mom and dad are going to help you with Parker, always. When you go off to college or if you decide to stay in Memphis for school, take their help. You and I are finished, but we are connected because of our son. I don't want to see you out there like that; at least I want to know that you graduated high school and my name should be on that high diploma just as much as yours should be on that diploma. Rather you know it or not, Victoria, you got lucky with me."

Victoria looked at David in silence. This was her first time seeing him for the guy her brother and sisters tried to warn her about. He was so smooth with his rudeness that she didn't know rather or not to take it or fight back with words.

She batted her eyelashes and said, "David, my name will be on my high school diploma because I worked for it and earned it. Don't be a moron! Maybe if you're lucky you'll get your degree while you're up here, unless your mom has to come up and clean up your mess by talking to professors on your behalf and doing the work for you."

"Victoria, let's not talk about mothers. I don't want to argue with you, you came up here to try to hurt me by breaking up with me after all I've done for you. I'm trying my best to keep my composure while my mother is here and so I don't mess up my reputation around campus." David replied.

Victoria walked away, but just as she was turning her back David grabbed her by the arm and asked "What are we fighting about? And why are you dumping me? Nobody said a long distant relationship was easy, I told you if you stay with me it'll work out in the end for you. Trust me, please be patient…Victoria."

"David, you just told me that you're the reason I'm going to graduate high school and your name should be on my diploma." Victoria replied.

"I said it out of anger, you know two names can't fit on that diploma?! Stop playing!" David said with laughter, trying to get Victoria to smile at his jokes.

This time Victoria didn't laugh, she was starting to see David had another personality that she somehow never got to see. He walked with her to the bookstore and bought her a few school items and jerseys with his name on it. He introduced her to some faculty and told them that she was his fiancé and smart enough to come here next year for their nursing program. Of course Victoria smiled and took it all in, but on the insides she thought who have I been dating for all these years? He comes home bearing gifts to keep me silent. He's always charming and making me laugh. He's a great family man when we're together and around his family. When we argue he's the first to make up and try to make me compromise with whatever he says. I feel like a puppet that has learned to adjust to his scenes.

CHAPTER 6

It wasn't long before this ambitious praying girl, decided to listen to her friend's advice and take a walk on the bad side. Although she knew Christy's household was different from hers, she worried for herself because if she got caught she would be back with her sisters and that wasn't a good environment for a 17 year old senior in high school with a son. She started to date this 21 year old senior that played football at Worchester Jr. College and everything about him was nice when David wasn't, his name was Joey but everybody called him Joy. He didn't live on campus and had a nice spot in downtown Memphis. He always took Victoria to his fraternity parties; she started to socialize with his friends and made new friends in the process. Christy was right there along the way and they always had a blast together.

Victoria eventually ended up quitting her job after school. Joy convinced her that it was too much on a single mom to work and go to school. He would always bash David and say things like what type of man would leave his woman and son to have his parents do his job. He gave Victoria a key to his place and told her that she and Parker were welcome to come by anytime when she wanted to get out of that house. Christy would always tease her about getting boxes for her big move to Joy's place, but Victoria was slightly torn on wanting to be this good girl that pleased everyone verses living her life and going with the flow of change.

~

"Victoria, I was in the mall today and I wanted something to eat. I went to your job and didn't see you, baby. So I had a little talk with your boss and he said that you quit your job weeks ago. Victoria, are you prostituting like your sisters?" Mrs. Tucker asked.

"WHAT?!" Victoria shouted, "Mrs. Tucker, please don't talk about my sisters. You are way out of line and maybe I am way out of line for living here as long as I have. It's time for me and Parker to move out. I won't ever keep him away from you all, but I need to live and enjoy my life." Victoria explained.

"Sweetheart, you're 17 years old with a 3 year old and no job. Where on earth are you going to go?" Mrs. Tucker said.

"Back home with my sisters, where I need to be and what my mom would have wanted is for us to stick together. I'm not insignificant and I know how to stay on top of my school work, I'll make it." Victoria explained.

Mrs. Tucker took a seat and started to speak calmly to Victoria, "I know you'll make it, young lady. Why do you think I held on to you for so long, because my son needs a strong young lady like you to keep him going in the right direction? Although I know at times I'm out of line, but Victoria I love you and Parker because we're family. If you really need to go, you leave and Parker stays."

Victoria laughed, "Mrs. Tucker, that's not an option. My son comes with me, but like I said you can see him whenever." Victoria left the room to call Christy. She brought boxes over and together they started to pack.

Christy whispered, "Are you moving in with Joy?"

"Yes! I don't have to take this....I deserve better." Victoria replied.

"Have you told him?" Christy asked.

"No, I figured I'll surprise him. He gave me a key." Victoria said.

Christy laughed and replied, "Um…you may want to call Joy and talk first. I taught you better than that! Don't be a fool and show up unannounced."

Once they finished packing everything, they headed to the house where her sisters lived to call Joy. When she arrived at the house, the kitchen was a mess; in fact, the entire house smelled awful. She called Joy and left him several voicemails, but he didn't answer and never called back. Christy helped Victoria clean the house, she figured she better clean up if her and her son where going to be spending the night in the house. Kel was in her room with a man and Tia was nowhere to be found.

While cleaning, Christy told her, "He's going to call back tomorrow; I bet he's out with his boys. Don't panic!"

Victoria laughed and replied in a facetious tone, "Yeah, I'm not panicking this is the perfect environment for me and my son. Tia's drugs are on the coffee table, while Kel's bedroom has turned into a brothel."

Christy and Victoria both laughed, Victoria added, "I have to laugh to keep from crying when it comes to my family."

"Yes, you do and you always keep a smile on your face through it all. That's what makes you strong and unique, Victoria. I never told you this, but I'm sorry when you got pregnant and I along with the other cheerleaders pushed you away from our table. I told my mom how you just kept on coming to school and held your head up through it all. I told her how you continued with all of your other activities at school and didn't let social cliques stop you. That's what made me stay in touch with you, because I refused to lose a great friend for a lifetime to have temporary acceptance by the cheerleading squad at school." Christy said.

Victoria replied with a smirk, "You know I wanted to hit you right?! I thought this girl is my best friend just like family and you were putting the cheerleading squad before me. Then I thought to myself, she just wants that co-captain position so I'll let her work. You know if I didn't have Parker that would have been my spot."

Christy replied jokingly and said, "Oh whatever, Victoria… please your toe touches were always off."

Both of them laughed and hugged before being interrupted by Parker joining in on the hug.

Christy said, "Come on, son…come to daddy!"

Victoria laughed so loud that she woke Kel, and said to Christy "Oh don't get me wrong, David's a good dad when he's in town… my son has a dad."

She could here Kel telling her guest where the restroom was and then she entered Victoria's room.

"For a minute I thought momma was here. The house smells so good, are you going to cook too?" Kel asked.

Christy laughed and left out of the room with Parker.

Victoria replied, "No, sis I'm not going to cook…I only cleaned the house. You know you could do this before having any company over?"

Kel replied, "Victoria, don't come in here trying to run things. I do clean up…good night; I'm going back to my room."

Before Kel could go back in her room, her male guest spotted Victoria's face.

"Oh, you're David's fiancé?" the male guest said, before Kel grabbed him and pulled him back to her room.

Victoria smiled and mumbled to herself, nope now I'm Joy's girl. She thought to herself, am I turning into one of my sisters? Have I lost my voice as being a strong, ambitious, driven, young determined girl and turned into every other guy's toy? If I sit nice and quiet like a lady should then I'd be another Mrs. Tucker, but if I decide to live my life to the fullest with my best friend Christy then I'll get labeled.

A double standard does exist; women can't do what
men do without getting a name for themselves.

Christy came back into the room and said, "Please stop sitting there thinking and talking to yourself. I'm glad you don't do that in front of people, they're going to think you're weird! You've got options boo; you're a Basketball wife/Football lady all in one state. You lucky little lady and you're my best friend. Whew! I'm heading home; call me tomorrow when you're ready to move your stuff in your condo in downtown Memphis!"

~

The next day, Brittany called to lecture Victoria on why she should stay at the Tucker's until she graduates high school. At this point, Joy still hasn't returned Victoria's phone call. Everything Brittany has said to her is playing heavy on her mind and the last thing she wants to do is call Mrs. Tucker to return to this lady's house. She did make an effort to call her to let Parker speak to his grandparents and went over to pick up a few of Parker's things.

Mrs. Tucker greeted Victoria at the door with a hug, "You know I love you, just like my daughter. My door is always open for you."

Victoria replied, "Thank you, Mrs. Tucker. I really appreciate everything you and Mr. Tucker have done for me."

"Call me momma, dear. I know you appreciate our help. My son told me to have you call him whenever you came back to get the last of your things." Mrs. Tucker replied.

Victoria left Parker in the room with his grandmother and went outside to make a phone call to David. Apart of her felt like, if your mom told you that I was leaving their house why didn't he put forth an effort to call me first to check on his son?

David answered his phone, "My future wife, trying to break bad."

"Hi, David." Victoria replied.

"So you are going back to the house with your sisters? You don't want to listen to me….this is a man's world, Victoria." David laughed and continued talking, "So you think a 21 year old that's in the first round draft pick for the NFL, Mr. Joy, is going to take it serious with you, you're just something new and nice for him to flaunt around his frat brothers and classmates. Keep listening to clueless Christy and you can hang up your dreams of going to college."

Victoria sat quiet on the phone and thought, how in the world does he know about Joy. The only thing she could do was deny, deny, deny.

"Joy, who are you talking about?! Who's in the first round draft pick for the NFL?" Victoria replied and thought to herself, Joy never told me he was in the first round draft for the NFL. He never mentions too much about football, he only speaks about his fraternity brothers.

David laughed and said, "You suck at being bad, you're going to always be my baby. Don't play dumb with me, Victoria because that's going to upset me. Now move your stuff and my son's stuff back into the house with my parents. I'll be home next weekend; if you're not there I'm coming to get my son."

Victoria hung up the phone and went into the house to get Parker. She gave the phone back to his mother; she left with her head up high and smile on her face.

"Bye, Mrs. Tucker. I'll call Monday morning before I drop Parker off on my way to school." Victoria said before leaving out of the door.

Later that evening, Joy called her. Victoria figured since David thought he knew something of what was going on between them and she kept silent on that one that she would do the same to Joy. She was a little upset, but she looked at it as an opportunity to use him. She was taking her anger out on Joy, instead of David.

A woman should love people and use things.

"Hey, boo I was expecting to see you in my place when I made it home last night." Joy said.

"Really, I was a little busy with Parker. It won't happen again, babe. What are you doing?" Victoria replied in a contemptuous tone.

"Getting ready to watch this football game. Are you going to use your key? You can bring Parker." Joy replied.

Victoria thought long and hard, rather or not she should tell him or mention David's name to Joy but she didn't want to mess anything up.

"Yes, we're on our way." Victoria replied.

"Good, I have some food in the kitchen that I need you to cook." Joy said jokingly, "No, I'm kidding I'm not like that...we can cook together."

This was the first guy Victoria brought Parker around. She made it over, but he was asleep. On the inside, she was happy because she could finally let her hair down. His condo downtown had a beautiful view of the Mississippi river. Joy definitely had a bachelor's pad, and Victoria looked around there was no evidence of previously having a woman in his space. She went into the kitchen, her and Joy started preparing food together to eat while they watched the game. She was really enjoying this moment, she felt so free and lifted like an adult but she was only 17 years old. She realized that she never talked to him about her living situation and how she might need to move in with him. Apart of her felt ashamed that she would ask him for something like a place to stay just because he offered her the keys to his place. She started to compare herself with these independent mature women he had introduced her to at the fraternity parties and after the football games. She felt insignificant in his big world. Yes, to her friend and family she was admired and viewed as the responsible, driven, hardworking one but in his field she was just a teen mom.

One should guard their hearts and minds from comparison,
offense, hard heart, heaviness, and pride.

After the game went off Joy and her sat on the sofa and just looked out the window. He turned off all of the lights and pulled his sofa closer to the huge windows for them to enjoy the view. Joy never tried anything with Victoria, not even before he gave her the key to his place. He just told her that he would be there for her and Parker to help whenever he could. He also said she was a great listener and he could talk to her about anything, he doesn't have many friends that he can confide in about obstacles in life. Victoria fell asleep in his arms. The next morning they both woke by the sunrise. Since he was always making Victoria feel special with small gestures, she decided to cook him breakfast. He went into his room and got Parker up, he told her that he'll get him cleaned up for her while she's cooking. He started to wash Parker's clothes and ran his bath water. Victoria stood there in the kitchen speechless. It was the little things, the little help from a helping hand that she had never gotten from David that made her view Joy from another perspective. She had to tell him about what David said, she was curious to know how they even knew of each other and/or if they knew one another.

"How tough is your skin, Victoria?" Joy asked.

"Well I guess it's pretty tough." Victoria answered still in shock by everything David was doing for her and Parker.

"Do you want to know why I gave you my key?" Joy replied.

"To use it and come over right?" Victoria replied.

"Yes and to move you in dear. You have a sister named Brittany in nursing school right?" Joy asked.

"Yes, how do you know my sister? And move me in?" Victoria asked, although in her mind she knew she was in no position to have too much pride not to move in with him.

"Yes, move you in. I know of Brittany from the nursing program at the community college. She's really smart and going to make a great nurse someday, you two are just alike. She's dating one of my frats." Joy replied.

"So you only wanted to date me because you knew of my sister? That's why you asked if my skin is tough…oh wow, like I'm a charity case." Victoria asked.

"No, sweetheart, I started dating you because I like you and see your drive as a teen mom. I met your sister at one of my frat brothers' weddings; she was there with my other frat brother. Memphis is small, your last name is rare and both of your faces look alike. I asked him if his girlfriend had any sisters and he told me about Tia, Brittany, and you. That's why I gave you my key so soon because he told me a little more about your situation and I want to help you. I asked if you had tough skin, because I'm not perfect but I'm a good guy just trying to help you out since I'm in a position to help out." Joy explained.

Victoria stood in silence. Joy started to set the bar on his kitchen island and picked Parker up to sit on the barstool. They all ate breakfast and he told Victoria that he would help her get her things packed and out of the Tucker's house.

"Well, thank you Joy. I kind of already packed and moved my stuff out of the Tucker's house the other night. I'm back at the house with my sisters." Victoria replied.

"Oh, yeah we got to get your stuff over here ASAP. I'm shocked they still have the house. And you're welcome dear." Joy replied.

After a few days, Joy's downtown condo had transformed from a bachelor's pad to a family spot. A part of Victoria felt like she was putting herself in some bad situations to depend on men, instead of trusting and depending on God. There was always something in her, stopping her from just letting go and not worrying about consequences. Victoria was hard on herself, because she knew she needed to graduate high school to advance to college because it would open more doors for her future endeavors.

We can plan our life out the way we want it to go, but
God's plans for our life is so much more rewarding.

~

Brittany found out Victoria was living with Joy, she was upset but knew his place was better for her than the Tucker's house since Victoria and David were no longer together. She also knew she didn't want Victoria back at home with Tia and Kel. She would always give her big sister advice and just tell her to take it slow with Joy, keep the friendship and lines of communication open. Brittany had matured and learned so much just from being exposed to a new environment and new peers in nursing school. She was now in a position to be a big sister and able to mentor Victoria.

CHAPTER 7

*God won't give you everything you want, but you can trust
God to give you the very best that he has for you.*

Kel was the sister that Ryan kept in touch with while he was
incarcerated. He would write her and make phone calls to her,
because she was the one home most of the time. Ryan's sentence
could have been reduced, but the cousins that were responsible for
paying the lawyer didn't keep their end of the deal with payment
arrangements. Unfortunately, for Ryan he got the short end of the
stick and had to do his time. This was stressful on him, but it made
him turn to his sisters instead of having his cousins take care of his
financial obligations. Kel tried to visit Ryan and send money as much
as possible; she tried cleaning up her act with the frequent trips out
of town and the plethora of male guests, because her brother needed
her. However, she was in no position to help Tia. This was the sister
that needed the most help, yet no one knew where to start with her.

Tia was the oldest and suffered from substance abuse. From the
little their mom shared with Tia and Kel about their dad, he was
never a drug user so this habit Tia formed wasn't a generational curse.

However, the fast paced lifestyle with different men was something Tia got from their mother.

In order to break generational curses one must make a conscious effort on your own to make a change in your habits and lifestyle.

Instead it was something she started, because of the company she kept around her. The drug use started small in social gatherings with drinking and having a little marijuana, then it led to her taking pills, and eventually experimenting with other drugs to help boost her high. Most nights Tia didn't come home and for days she would be missing. When she would return home, she never stayed long and would always be accompanied by a lot of women and one man in particular. Kel hated to see his face, because he was so controlling over Tia and because of this no one could reason with her.

Meanwhile, in Tia's world she was always in someone's VIP booth at the club in the latest fashions. She kept herself up, always looking fierce; that's why her drug habits were hard to spot because she didn't appear as your typical drug user. Her boyfriend was this well-known pimp and drug dealer, but he was never in Memphis long because he was always on the road. He was extremely protective of Tia, because he knew Tia had made him a lot of money in the past so he always had to be seen with her on his arm. Since none of the girls grew up with a father in their lives, it was obvious they all had a similar pattern with men. They all ran to men looking for love, his ability to provide, and protection…something they missed growing up. Instead of being patient and allowing the right man that had those same qualities to find them.

Never look in zeal, be patient for it's a virtue.

Aside from family matters, Kel was extremely busy with doing hair. Her clientele was starting to build and she was thankful for the source of income she was bringing in. She had finally decided to go back to school to actually obtain her hair license so that she could work in a salon. She would always joke with her clients and say that maybe one day she'll own her own salon. Until that day would ever come, she was content with styling hair in the house since she was the one left there most of the time.

Behind bars, Ryan fought for his manhood. He would write Kel long letters just explaining how he felt about being incarcerated and fighting just to stay alive in prison. During his phone calls to Kel, he would always say that he would have never gotten into trouble had he stayed home with his sisters. He said chasing fast money is what got him into mischief, now he has a criminal record and it's going to be impossible to have a bright future like he would have had before. Kel would always try to keep Ryan encouraged and speak some type of life into him. She could feel it in Ryan's voice that he was losing faith, but most importantly down on his luck and himself. Although Ryan did make bad choices, he got himself into more trouble than he had bargained for and it changed his entire life upside down. Ryan felt like a failure, he wasn't the man for their household anymore and he couldn't be there for his sisters. This took away something in his manhood; he no longer felt like a man. This was hard for Kel to relate to, because a woman can't teach a man how to be the man for his family. Kel would always try to pick his spirits up just by giving him encouraging words, because she hated seeing her brother down like that. Eventually, Ryan crossed paths with a great mentor in prison who was Muslim and he started to teach Ryan about God. Although Kel would joke with her brother about joining a nation he knew nothing about. She also feared who he was in contact with, she obviously figured with him in prison it was best to be mentored by a Muslim than a prison gang member that may have brought trouble his way

Brittany had finally graduated from the nursing program, she was officially Nurse Brittany. Victoria and Kel came to her graduation and they had an opportunity to meet her boyfriend, Morris. Followed by the graduation, he planned a surprise dinner for Brittany and proposed to her. Everyone was so happy for her and of course she accepted it. Victoria thought to herself, what took Brittany so long to introduce him to her family. Was she ashamed of her family? This gentleman came from a really wealthy family and a standard household with a mom and dad. Victoria wanted to talk to her sister in private and ask why they were so late hearing about Morris and them getting that serious after they've dated for so long. Of course, this wasn't the time or place to discuss a sisters bond.

~

Meanwhile in Victoria's life, her and Joy had a wonderful friendship. She had one more semester until her high school graduation and Parker was growing and learning so much from Joy. He would take him to football camp with him and he played with some of the coaches' children just to give Victoria time alone to study. Joy finally came around to tell Victoria about him being in the first round draft for the NFL, he never made the cut. Most of his fraternity brothers would joke with him and say things like he really did, but just didn't want to leave M-town. Of course, Joy would always assure them that if he made it….he would have been out of Memphis!

The closer Victoria got with Joy, the more she learned about his childhood and upbringing. She had a better understanding of why he took her in so fast. He grew up in the foster care system, always bouncing from house to house. His biological mother was a victim murdered from domestic violence by his father. Joy had to go live with his grandmother, years later she passed away and he was placed in group home for holding until he was later placed in his foster home. For years his father got away with his mom's murder and still lived in Memphis. After enough investigating they closed the case. It wasn't until years later; he killed his fiancé due to domestic violence that they connected him to the murder of Joy's mother. He now spends the rest of his life in prison.

To Joy football was his passion and running on the field was his way of running from his hurt. Coaches knew his living situations would always change, so he never played football at his school because he never stayed at the same school for long. Instead he played in the community for different AAU teams. This way it was better for the coaches to keep a close eye on his performance. From the support and help of his coaches, he ended up getting a full ride scholarship to Worchester Jr. College where he played football. He would always tell Victoria that she was different from most girls he's dated, because she actually had a personality and he could talk to her. She had heard this before from David, and saw another side come from him when things didn't go his way. She took it all in, but kept the advice her big sister Brittany gave her which was to take it as a friendship and nothing personal.

Although Victoria and David weren't on the best of terms, they did manage to communicate for Parker's sake. They would meet at the Tucker's house, and to David, he never knew Victoria and his son were living with Joy and she never told him. As far as he knew, she was back at home with her sisters.

Mrs. Tucker stated, "Victoria, I heard about Brittany's graduation from nursing school. Tell her that I said congratulations and I'm proud of her. I'm proud of you too, sweetheart. Truthfully, I didn't know what you were going to do going back to your sister's house trying to finish high school and raise our boy."

Victoria smiled and replied, "Thank you, I'm trying…just taking it one day at a time and doing my best. I still have so much work to do."

David nodded and told her, "You probably have my mom fooled with thinking you're making it and able to take care of yourself and my son. But I know you're up to something and you're no good. Like I told you before my name belongs on that diploma just as much as yours."

Victoria knew the best way to fight David was not with words or actions simply ignore him without adding fuel to his fire. For an 18 year old teen mom, Victoria was poised as a young lady and knew when to exit.

Motherhood, responsibilities, and life itself had pruned Victoria.

Kel received a call from the police station, it was Tia.

Tia sobbed and tried to speak between her tears, "Kel, I....need you....to come get me."

Kel replied, "Where are you, Tia? What's wrong? I'll come get you."

Tia was crying hysterically before a female officer picked up the phone to speak to Tia.

"Hello, my name is Officer Clarke. May I ask whom I'm speaking with?" the officer asked.

"This is Kelsie, Tia's sister." Kel replied.

"Ok, let me explain the situation. Your sister was at Club Hot tonight and the gentleman she was with got into an altercation with the owner of the club. The fight was bad; to the point officers stripped the car he was in when he tried to leave. They found drugs and weapons. Your sister was in that car with him. Now luckily, she had me and my partner who were nice enough to bring her back to the station instead of driving her downtown. My question to you, are you able to come pick your sister up and keep her nose clean and away from that boy? He's looking at doing some time, after they're done investigating." the officer stated.

Kel listened in silence and was angry because she knew that boy was trouble, "Yes, mamm I'll come get my sister. Which precinct are you at?"

Kel took down the address and headed to get Tia. She called to let Brittany know what was going on, but her fiancé Morris answered the phone and told her that she was sleeping. Next, she called Victoria and informed her that she'll keep her posted on everything going on. Joy told Victoria that she was a senior in high school and her mind should be on prom, graduation, planning for college, ACT scores, and enjoying time with friends' not family drama. Although Victoria wanted to focus on her situation, at the time she couldn't…it was always like this for her. She worried for her family, her sisters was all she had for family. Joy would explain to Victoria that Brittany isolated herself away from her family for a little while, just to graduate and take care of her business. He would always tell Victoria that's what she's going to have to learn to do if she wants to make it in life.

When Kel arrived at the precinct to pick up Tia, she barely recognized her sister. Her face was swollen and eyes were blood shot red, her clothes were damaged like she had been fighting. Although the officer told Kel one side of the story, she knew Tia had more to share with her. When they got in the car, before Kel could ask Tia cried and held her sister. On the ride home, she told her that her and her boyfriend where sitting at the bar because they didn't have a booth ready for them. He became upset because he was supposed to have a booth that night. She said she wasn't sure if he had too much to drink prior to the club, but he started to fight the bartender then security and the club owner got involved. She was scared for her life when weapons where pulled out and shots were fired, by the time she made it out of the crowd and pulled the car around. She explained to Tia what happened to her face, he beat her in the car because she didn't fight in the club with him. He told her that she needed to walk home and find her own way out here, because he was done with her. Shortly after he was pointed out by the club security and was arrested. The female police officer knew Kel had nothing to do with it, but was in the wrong place at the wrong time and with the wrong person so she took her to the precinct to call for her ride home.

Kel remained speechless while she listened to Tia explain her story.

"Tia, Ryan wrote me a letter a few weeks ago talking about change. The only way one can seek change, is if they go after something different from what they've done in the past. I'm saying that to say this, Tia has to want to change her life around for Tia's sake." Kel said.

Tia replied while whipping her tears away, "Kel, I have no other choice but to change. What do I have left? He was all I knew and he gave me life."

At that moment, Kel stopped the car and became upset with her sister's words.

Kel said, "No man can give you life, God gave you life when he created you sister. Now your life can somehow go down on a spiraled downfall of chaos and negativity, after years of surrounding yourself with that. But you'll be just fine once you get off the drugs and figure out what Tia wants to do with her life and get your life back. Yes, it's time for Tia to make a change because that's what's best for you."

Tia nodded her head and hugged her sister to say, "You're right, Kel."

Days later, Kel called a family meeting and wanted her sisters over to sit down and talk with Tia. She updated them on Ryan's situation and also found it necessary to figure out how all of them will help Tia get the best help possible.

"Let's go to church." Victoria suggested.

"So many times people run to church with their problems, Victoria. Tia has to want to change for Tia, the change starts from within." Brittany argued.

"We haven't been to church as a family since m⌐
Kel added.

"I don't think church is the answer, that's the plac⌐
will be judged and ridiculed." Tia said.

"My point exactly! We can pray all day and run to ch⌐
all of our problems. We have common sense and are capable of
using those resources without running to church for direction and
guidance. You need rehab to kick your drug habit. I found a great
place on the bulletin board at school and I'll give you the name of it
later this week." Brittany added.

Victoria observed Brittany's know it all demeanor on how she
shot down the idea of going to church and just started to pay more
attention to her sister's actions and words.

"It wouldn't hurt to still go to church as a family." Victoria added.

"Yes, that's fine we can go to church as a family." Brittany replied
in an annoyed tone. "Maybe later once Tia is clean and much
better. Just as if mom was still living, but we don't need to go as the
helpless sisters lost in this world. We can put our heads together; get
our mind right and work to make a difference on ourselves first."
Brittany added.

All of the sisters agreed, this was only the beginning for them.
It had been a long time since they all got together to talk and lay
things out. It has also been the first time they all decided it was time
to hold one another hands to help pull each other up verses living in
their own secluded world.

*God promised to show love to a thousand generations of those
who love him and keep his commandments. Exodus 20:6*

CHAPTER 8

Finally, Victoria was happy that her sisters and she were making strides together. They haven't been on one accord since their mom passed away. Even when she was living they weren't as close as they should have been.

When things fall apart, work at the problem don't just pray about it.
It'll come together with much better results.

Tia had gotten the help she needed with her drug and men addiction to bring her to sobriety. She struggled financially and wasn't able to find work with no prior work experience. She would listen to lectures from Brittany on going to a trade school. However, Kel would always assure her to take it easy because she didn't want to see her sister go back out in the streets chasing fast money. Kel was really marketing her hair profession and becoming very successful in the hair industry. If she did travel, she was traveling to do hair shows to gain more clientele for work.

While everything was going well for her sisters, Victoria was unhappy with her living situation. It seemed as if her welcome was worn out with Joy, because she noticed a change in him. He stopped doing so much for her and her son; he also didn't always come home some weekends. Victoria knew that it was time for her to leave. She needed to find her own path and make it with Parker on her hip. Christy would always call her crazy for wanting to leave a friend as great as Joy.

Victoria decided to sit down and talk to Joy to let her know she was planning to move back in with her sisters.

"Joy, I have to tell you thank you so much for all that you've done. With letting me and my son come live with you and just being a friend. Thank you! I needed that change of scenery." Victoria stated.

"You're welcome, I told you that I'm not perfect but I want to help you as much as possible. Why are you talking as if you're leaving?!" Joy asked.

"Because I start college in the fall and I want to be sure that my living arrangements are contingent. I know most nights you don't come home and I just want to be sure you have your space and privacy back as well." Victoria explained before she was interrupted.

"Did I tell you that it was a problem with you living here? Did I say I needed my space back?" Joy stated in a stern demeanor. "I don't get you women, I opened up to you something I haven't done with any woman. Gave you a key because I trusted you, and I wanted to help you out and when you're done with me you're ready to leave. So I guess you're back with David now?" Joy asked.

Victoria thought this handsome college football player and well-known fraternity brother is upset that I'm trying to leave him. He could have any woman he wants, so why would he be upset. She thought to herself in most cases he seems annoyed by my presence, I can't reach this man mentally. I have no clue what he's going through, but I know I want my son to be in a stable home. Victoria bouncing from man to man wasn't her idea of stability.

"Joy, I guess I just thought that you needed your space back and I was trying to get back with my sisters." Victoria tried to explain before being interrupted again by Joy.

This time he was really upset, "Victoria, good luck sweetheart. I tried to help you, just like David and his family tried to help you. If you really think you're going to graduate college living with Kel and Tia…you're not going to make it, you'll end up as another statistic."

Joy's words alone cut and hurt, it was that moment that Victoria pulled out motivation to press forward to a new beginning with her sisters. By the end of the night, she packed her and Parker's things and was back at the house with her sisters. For once, Victoria finally felt like she was home with her family and felt so comfortable and at ease. Although her sister's and she previously had their spats and disagreements, they were mending their relationships and she was happy to see their bonds being reconnected.

For once, none of the sisters were dating and were all trying to help the bride-to-be prepare for her wedding along with bettering themselves.

Victoria noticed how Brittany kept Morris and his family very sacred and away from her sisters. When they would have dinners most of the time Brittany would only bring Victoria. When in the company of his family, Brittany would always speak up for Victoria when she was asked questions pertaining to housing or school. Victoria didn't like this; it was almost like her sister was trying to put on this façade in front of Morris and his family. While out shopping for bridal shower keepsakes, Victoria decided to address this issue.

"So darling, what college do you attend and what's your classification?" Victoria mocked in a snobbish voice.

Brittany paused and looked at her sister and said, "Stop that. It's not funny."

Victoria laughed and continued mocking Morris' mother, "Darling, how is motherhood treating you? Have you decided which preparatory program you will enroll Parker in next Fall? Time goes by fast, dear."

Brittany pushed Victoria and said, "It's not funny! Stop that."

Victoria continued taunting, "Oh sister darling, you have something on your nose."

Finally, Brittany spoke up to say "You know Victoria; if it wasn't for Morris and his family I don't know if I would have graduated nursing school. It was tough; I couldn't do it on my own. Of course to my sisters, I assured you that I had everything under control but it was so hard. I learned that God is our source that provides you with resources. I'm going to marry my resource; his family has been extremely resourceful with helping me get a job."

Victoria stopped teasing and replied, "I never knew you were struggling in school. You appeared as if you had it all together. But didn't you tell me that I allowed Mrs. Tucker to groom and refine me for David's sake. You talked a good game as if you would be there for me once you finished school."

Brittany replied, "In nursing school, nobody has it all together. It can be tough, that's why you have to have a support system and make friends with classmates. Victoria, I want to be there for you and Parker but things started moving so fast with Morris and me that I couldn't keep my promise."

Victoria nodded her head and said, "I understand. Sorry for teasing your mother in-law. But Brittany, every time she asked me a question you spoke up for me like I didn't know how to answer questions for myself. It was almost like you were afraid that I would embarrass you."

Brittany explained, "It wasn't that Victoria, you're my sister and I spoke so highly of you all. Tia has just started getting her life together and I wasn't sure if she was ready to meet them. While Kel busy working, I knew that you would come and be on your ɴavior."

ctoria set in silence taking in everything Brittany just said, ɪr or not she admits it she is embarrassed of her family and only wanted to show Victoria. Victoria started to question why wasn't she embarrassed of me? I'm a teen mom that has not provided a stable home for my son. Victoria started to view her glass, half empty and not half full. She started to doubt her own worth off her sister's behavior.

Never allow anyone's behaviors and actions to pull
you down to think negatively about yourself.
Always keep working to make improvements in your own life.

"Brittany, we probably should get back to shopping for your bridal keepsakes because I don't want to ruin the moment." Victoria said.

"Ruin the moment. Why did you say it like that? You know we always have debates and agree to disagree." Brittany replied.

This time this wasn't a debate, in Victoria's eyes, Brittany was ashamed of her family set up and where she came from. She was hiding the truth from Victoria, because Kel would have re-scheduled some hair appointments to meet Morris and his family. Just like Tia was sober enough to come around his family. Brittany had changed, she wasn't the same Brittany that she was before and Victoria didn't know how to address her.

Life has a way of growing us in the direction that
we're meant to grow in. During the process, you may
lose friends and family but never lose yourself.

"Brittany, do you love him?" Victoria asked. "I mean you said you were going to marry your resource, so do you love him."

"Victoria, don't ask rhetorical questions. I'm shopping for my bridal shower...do I love him?" Brittany laughed off in an unsure tone.

Victoria stopped and watched her sister, again paying attention to her words and actions.

Brittany cried in the store and replied, "No. I'm barely attracted to Morris. Have you seen him?!"

"So you're marrying him to use his family for their resources?" Victoria asked.

"Victoria, let's go. You're ruining my bride to-be moment. I can't even shop in peace and I love to shop! If you weren't my sister I would think that you're jealous." Brittany said while sobbing.

"Jealous...let's not go there sister, we've never had that type of relationship. You're strong, you have to be extremely strong to marry a man that you're not even mentally and physically attracted to let alone see yourself spending the rest of your life with. If you have a son, would you want your son to be like Morris? Would you want your son to marry a woman like you? That's only trying to use him." Victoria carried on as they got in the car.

"Victoria, shut the hell up. Let's change the subject." Brittany shouted.

"Damn, I guess there's no such thing as true love anymore." Victoria replied. "I mean that's how I looked at Joy and David, as opportunities to use them for the convenience of my son. Although I started off falling in love with them, it was lust. I can admit for an 18 year old single mother, I've never been in love. But I wouldn't be foolish enough to marry to please myself and marry for my resources. You would always tell me to use my voice and speak up for myself...I wish you would take your own advice."

Brittany continued to cry as they left the store and got in the car, she replied, "I wish I was strong enough to use my own voice, too. He'll be done with his PhD next Spring. And he wants to marry me, Brittany from the broken home and pushed her way through to graduate from nursing school. He wants to spend the rest of his life with me? Why would I be foolish enough to call that off and let him get away from me? I have a chance to have a family of my own with a doctor. If I have children, they'll have a mom and dad in the same household. Come on Victoria, a black doctor married to a black nurse in Memphis. We would be a black power couple. I will be able to afford to really support you and Parker while you go through nursing school."

Victoria dropped her mouth as she took in everything her sister just said.

Victoria replied, "Yep, you're one of those now."

"What?" Brittany asked.

"Go ahead…get your family with the white picket fence. You deserve it sister. Even if it's not real love, you can grow to love him… right?! Let me guess, because it's the American Dream. You're willing to live a lie." Victoria replied in a facetious tone.

Brittany pulled the car over and asked Victoria to drive. She was obviously having a moment in the backseat and just needed to cry.

"You, you can grow to love someone. I don't know, Victoria. For once, I don't have any answers for my own situation." Brittany said.

"Sometimes it's ok to be lost or not have answers for your own situation. When things are broken, you can step back and really examine your own situation. Just to lighten the mood, he has girly hips. Would you want your son to have girly hips like him?" Victoria added.

Brittany burst into laughter and stopped crying so much. "That man has hips like his mother!"

"You don't have to tell me, I saw." Victoria added.

They both stopped laughing and decided to drive to a restaurant. This was a great day to have some lunch and drinks with her sister. While in the restaurant, they continued their conversation.

"You know you have to figure out a way to call off that engagement?" Victoria said.

"I know, his family is going to be so upset with me. But I have to do what's best for Brittany. Ugh this is so hard, if I let Dr. Morris…." Brittany stated before Victoria interrupted her.

"Stop calling him by his title, because every time you do that you're only going to make it harder on you making a decision of letting go of a doctor. If you're not in love, then I wouldn't marry. Start a friendship first, and keep that going for a while. If he comes off pushy for marriage then you may want to talk with him so that you both are on the same page. Communication is key. No bride to-be should walk down the aisle with a man that she doesn't really love and you're not attracted to him. That has to be heartbreaking." Victoria replied.

"See Victoria, that's something I've always admired about you. You were never afraid to speak up to David even when you lived with the boy's mom. Although you were extremely hard on yourself, you weren't afraid to be seen on the arm of a college athlete and fraternity man like Joy. Every lady on just about all the college campus in Tennessee wants some Joy in their life. You know how he got that nickname, right?" Brittany rambled on.

"Wow! No I don't know why he got that nickname; I never got Joy in that way." Victoria added.

"What?! He moved you into his place and you didn't sleep with him? You two were really friends?" Brittany asked.

"Yes, we were really friends. He opened up to me about a lot of his childhood, but after a few months living there he started to keep a distance as if my welcome was worn out. Don't get me wrong, I did want him in that way but I was too afraid to make the move because he was Joy the college athlete." Victoria replied.

"Have you talked to him since you left?" Brittany asked.

"Not really, he told me if I moved back into the house with Tia and Kel that I would be another statistic. Words hurt; I don't think I want to talk with him again. It's not what he said, it's just how he said it." Victoria replied.

"Yeah, that was low. Talking about my sisters like that...he has a lot of nerve. You might have actually let a good one get away. He probably really did like you and was saying that out of anger, because he wanted to help you, since he never slept with you. Joy doesn't really give to women, he takes from women. I don't know about that one, Victoria." Brittany added.

"But Brittany, look how possessive men can get when they feel like they're helping you. They treat you like you're their possession and belong to them. They want you to lose your voice and character. It shouldn't be that way and I don't want to live that way, I'm only 18 years old and Parker needs a stable home. Let me finish school and I'll show you the woman I can be for my son." Victoria added.

"You don't have to finish school to show me. I know you're a strong smart young lady, which has grown through a lot...you don't have to prove anything to me. Here I am Nurse Brittany and only wanting to marry for the look of a young power couple in Memphis. But if I had a doctor whew, think of how much shopping I could do..." Brittany replied.

"Yep, shop away that pain sister. At least you'll be dressed to impress and on the inside hurting because you're living a lie." Victoria replied.

Both sisters enjoyed each other's company and continued having lunch.

CHAPTER 9

Since Tia struggled to find work in Memphis, she was becoming very domesticated around the house. She always kept the place clean and dinner was always on the table. She decided to keep their house, looking like a home since all the sisters were back together. She was also Parker's nanny since all the other girls were busy working women.

Brittany had called off her engagement and even had to transfer hospitals. Somebody should have told her what she was getting herself into when you take help from the wrong people. Morris and his family tried to drag her name through the mud in the medical industry. She decided it was best to move back home with her sisters. Lucky for her nurses are in high demand so it wasn't long before she found another job.

Kel's clientele was growing extremely fast, too fast for her to do hair out of the house. She found a really nice salon not far from their house and began working there. She had saved up so much money from doing hair at the house for years. She was eager to buy her own salon, but Brittany convinced her to wait until she's financially prepared to own her own business. She also gave her some contacts

reat entrepreneurs in Memphis to help her learn a little
t being self-employed.

a struggled in nursing school. This was not as easy as
.. ..ged. She took Brittany's advice and even made friends with
classmates that formed study groups. She just wasn't getting the
material nor passing the test. After one semester of nursing school
and only 1 passing grade, she dropped out before being suspended.
She decided to talk to Brittany about her future endeavors.

"Brittany, I don't think nursing is the profession for me. I didn't
excel academically like I thought I could. That's rare for me and
a low blow, because I'm always making passing grades." Victoria
stated.

"Yes, nursing school is tough even when you buckle down in the
books. It can still be challenging. Remember how I struggled going
from one school to another not sure about my future endeavors.
Before enrolling in nursing school, it takes time." Brittany replied.
"Take some time off and give some time to Victoria and Parker."

"Yes, you're absolutely right." Victoria replied. "I love you,
Brittany."

"Love you, too, sister. You'll find out what you want to do just
give it time." Brittany replied.

*What works for someone else, may not work for you.
Find your own path, if you can't find it…create your own path!*

~

Victoria got a job working as a financial representative at a bank;
she enjoyed it because she met so many different people. She also
started to make professional friendships with some of the members.
The pay was comfortable for her and Parker, so she rarely put forth
an effort to think about higher education. Although Brittany would
keep it on her mind that she needs to go to college, Victoria had
gotten comfortable where she was employed. After about two years

working at this bank, it wasn't long before the bank downsized and outsourced her position. Here she was unemployed, but luckily her circumstances weren't that bad because she had her sisters to fall back on in the household.

CHAPTER 10

Victoria felt uneasy about her future endeavors, for once she didn't know. This young ambitious, goal-oriented girl that traveled down some roadblocks with bad love while on her journey to success was not successful. She wasn't working in her field, because she had dropped out of nursing school. She thought she had it all figured out. One day her and Christy went to lunch, this conversation made her re-examine her path in life.

"Victoria, the scholar…the smart girl that never messes up on anything. She's got all the advice for everyone's situation, but can't find her own path." Christy said jokingly.

"It's not funny, Christy. But go on…throw it at me. I deserve it!" Victoria said.

"No, nobody deserves to have their face in the mud. I promise I'm kidding and only saying it out of love. To get to this, when was the last time you spoke to Joy." Christy asked.

"I haven't, when I left he was very distant and told me that I'll be another statistic if I moved back in with my sisters. I don't want to keep repeating the negative stuff, but why did you ask?" Victoria replied.

"Well, from what I've heard from one of his fraternity brothers. He's in the process of opening up this mentoring program for troubled boys and girls. They say he grew up in foster care, I would have never known that about him." Christy said.

"Wow! I'm so happy for him and proud of him. He deserves the best with that. I want to go see him just to tell him congratulations, but he hasn't seen my face since the day I left and may not want to see me. I'll let him enjoy his moment." Victoria said.

"I don't know if he's enjoying his moment like that, word has it that he's single and cutting a lot of women off. He's really focused on that mentoring program. He could use a good counselor working at his center or business partner at his side. Since you always have the best advice and you're looking for a job." Christy replied.

"You have to have school and training to work in that profession. Besides I don't even understand how non-profits make their money. I'm ok, I'll find my own way. I have to Christy. You don't understand." Victoria explained.

"I understand sometimes you have too much pride for your own good." Christy argued.

"No, that's not having too much pride. That's learning that I don't want to be pulled around like a ragdoll and have my choices made for me and my son. I'm 19 years old now, back at home with my sisters and I'm a nursing school dropout. I need to find my own path for my future endeavors. I know I have to go back to school. Education is key and vital; it's something that no one can take away from me." Victoria said.

"You're right, Victoria….you're right…you're always right! But what if going into business with Joy could be your job while you go back to school?!" Christy explained.

"You still don't get it. You missed the point. It'll still put him in a position to feed me. He'll decide when I eat and that was the same environment I was in with David and his family. It's time I go to school, get in my profession and find my own path for Parker and myself." Victoria argued back.

"Well…excuse me for being a friend that didn't want you as the old maid with no man. I don't think Joy would be that arrogant as a business partner to cut you off like that. You're smart, he's smart and he opened up to you about his upbringing and you opened up to him. Working together could be the continuation of a great friendship." Christy said.

"I'm 19 years old; I'm far from being an old maid. I'm determined to make something of myself. Sometimes being broke, gives you your drive and adds fuel to your ambition. You can do it too, Christy. As for the continuation of Joy and I friendship and future endeavors as business partners…I don't know about that."

Victoria reversed the conversation and asked. "Come on, you're always talking about men. What do you want to do with your life? What are some of your career goals?"

Christy looked at Victoria with a stern look and replied, "Let's change the subject, I said you're right…you win the debate."

"It wasn't about a win or lose, I never knew it was a game. I asked my friend a question, I always knew you danced since we were children. But what do you want to be now that you're an adult, what is it that you want to do with your life?" Victoria said.

"Victoria, I work a job in retail. That's my dream job, my profession, and my career…I'm not like you so leave it alone. I date men and get money from them and enjoy my life. I work a little and play a little!" Christy replied.

"That's fun and it's nothing wrong with that. We're supposed to enjoy our life, work a little and play a little. But I know working a job in retail, that's all you want to do in life. Is that pay comfortable for you to sustain financially even when you're older." Victoria said.

"I'll make it financially comfortable." Christy replied with a firm tone.

"You're taking offense, but I know the dancer and employee in retail wants something more out of life for herself. It's not about dreaming aloud, it's about working with a passion in a field that you know you're meant to be in for the rest of your life!" Victoria said.

"Victoria, I've always wanted…that's ok, you're going to laugh." Christy said.

"No, I wouldn't! Tell me!" Victoria replied.

"I always wanted to open up my own dance studio, but I know I have to first start working at a local dance theatre helping the girls in dance. Or at least try to get my foot in the door, it's been 2 years since I've danced. Then I have to go to school for business…it's too much work." Christy said.

"Well sounds like we both have some work to do! Let's get to it." Victoria replied before fanning the waitress and said, "Waiter, check please!"

This is only the beginning….

49730651R00047

Made in the USA
Middletown, DE
21 June 2019